Story by Donna Warwick

Drawings by Dayne Sislen

GLASS PEN Press LLC
www.DonnaWarwickAuthor.com

We dedicate this book to our mothers, who made sure we ate our peas.

Published in the United States by Glass Pen Press LLC.

Visit us on the Web! www.DonnaWarwickAuthor.com
for a variety of teaching tools, crafts and
information on scheduling school visits.

Publication Data:
Warwick, Donna L.
There's a Mouse on My Head / by Donna Warwick ; Pictures by Dayne Sislen
Summary: A clever boy uses his imagination to avoid eating his peas.
His grandma and little sister join in the fun.
ISBN 978-0-9965615-0-1 (Hardcover), ISBN 978-0-9965615-1-8 (soft cover)
[1. Stories in Rhyme. 2. Behavior-Fiction. 3. Food Habits-Fiction.
4. Family Life-Fiction. 5. Mouse-Fiction] I. Sislen, Dayne, ill. II. Title.

There's a mouse on my head!
"I'm hungry," he said.
Please feed him my cheese
and please feed
him my bread!

His tummy is growling!
He wants all of these.
He wants you to feed him
my leftover peas!

"There's a mouse on your head!"
my grandmother said.
"I'll feed him your cheese
and I'll feed him your bread.

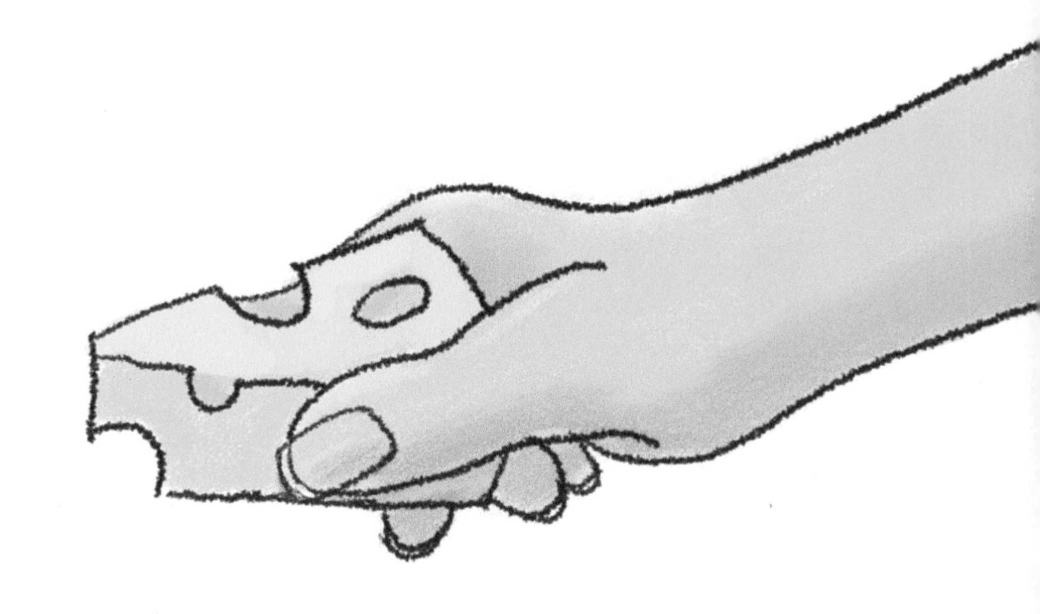

I’ll feed him your dinner
and when he is through,
I’ll just let him nibble
your cherry pie, too!”

But he doesn’t like cherries!
He doesn’t like pie!
Desserts make him dizzy!
Desserts make him cry!

I'll eat the pie for him!
I'll eat it up quick!
'Cause I don't want that mouse
on my head to get sick.

YICK!

EE

"There's a mouse on your
I heard Sister shriek,
and the poor startled mouse
gave a meek little "squeak."

EEK!"
squeak!

"He's eating your cheese!
He's eating your hair!"
screamed Sister who stood
on the seat of her chair.

“Let’s all eat our cheese
and let’s all eat our bread.
Let’s teach the mouse manners!”
our grandmother said.

"Two spoonfuls of peas
and two forkfuls of pie!"
Then Grandmother smiled
with a wink of her eye.

"Can I have a turn with that
mouse on your head?
Can I name him Nathan,
Lorenzo or **FRED**?

I'll teach him to pick up
my clothes and my toys!
Do dishes, feed fishes,
like other mouse boys!"

But he doesn't like work!
He doesn't like chores!
He hides in the corners!
He runs under doors!

He creeps into rooms and
you don't know he's there!
That's what a mouse likes!

He likes people to
SCARE!!

From his nest on my head
to a spoon that was clean,
he went BING and then

BOUNCED

off a bread trampoline.

He flipped through the air
with the greatest of ease,
then squeezed through the
cheese holes on his tiny knees.

He dribbled the peas,
even though some went
He STILL scored three points
in the bowl of the cat!

He juggled the cherries,
the cheese and the bread,
until he saw Grandmother
shaking her head.

"There's a mouse on your head,"
my grandmother said.
"Go teach him to brush his
mouse teeth
before bed.

Wash face and wash hands
and wash paws just like this!
Then come give your grandma
and sister a kiss."

There's a mouse on my head!
"*I'm sleepy,*" he said.
I'll give him a hug and
I'll put him to bed.

He says he'll be quiet.
He says he won't bite.
So, we're going to dreamland
and he says. . .

"Goodnight!"

CPSIA information can be obtained
at www.ICGtesting.com
Printed in the USA
LVHW07s2312290818
588621LV00007B/66/P